SUPER #2
GOOFBALLS

GOOfBalls in paradise

SUPER GOOFBALLS

Book One: That Stinking Feeling
Book Two: Goofballs in Paradise

SUPER GOOFBALLS #2

GOOFBALLS in Paradise

written and illustrated by
Peter Hannan

HarperTrophy®
An Imprint of HarperCollinsPublishers

This book is dedicated to Cole
(Amazing First-Born Dude).

Harper Trophy® is a registered trademark of
HarperCollins Publishers.

Library of Congress Cataloging-in-Publication Data
Hannan, Peter.
Goofballs in paradise / Peter Hannan. — 1st ed.
    p.   cm. — (Super goofballs ; bk. 2)
Summary: As Super Vacation Man sneaks off for a secret vacation,
Amazing Techno Dude and his pack of misfit superheroes must
defeat the grouchy supervillain Mondo Grumpo, and overcome his
special power, the evil finger shake of shame.
    ISBN-10: 0-06-085214-3 (trade bdg.)
    ISBN-13: 978-0-06-085214-6 (trade bdg.)
    ISBN-10: 0-06-085213-5 (pbk.)
    ISBN-13: 978-0-06-085213-9 (pbk.)
    [1. Heroes—Fiction. 2. Humorous stories.] I. Title.
PZ7.H1978Go 2007   2006019544
[Fic]—dc22   CIP
                                                          AC

TABLE OF CONTENTS

CHAPTER 1

Good Morning, Goofballs!

At 5:33 A.M. I was woken up by a series of superloud, superweird screams and shouts.

"AHHHHH-IIIIIII-EEEEEEE-AHHHHHHHHHHH!"

"EEEEEEEEEEEEEEKKK! ARGGGGGGGGGKT!"

"OOOOOOOO-EEEEEEEEEEE-NO-NO-NO-NO!"

This went on for a while.

It sounded like the end of the world.

But it wasn't.

Somebody had thrown
a moldy lemon in through
a window and it hit
T-Tex3000 on the head,
waking him up. And he
woke up grumpy. It was
a really nasty lemon.

T-Tex3000 isn't his full name. But I told him I was
a busy superhero who didn't have time to call him
"Super-Teeny-Tiny Tyrannosaurus-Tex 3000." He
followed me home yesterday after I accidentally time
traveled back to 65 million years B.C. He took a few
wrong turns in time and got a little mixed up. Also, he
shrank. A lot. He's about as big as a
hummingbird. A hummingbird-
sized space–cowboy–dinosaur–
superhero. Tiny, but he can

sure kick up a ruckus.

He had been having a nightmare about his terrifying time-travel trip, and when the lemon hit him, he thought he was passing through a meteor shower and panicked. He raced from room to room, waking up my other goofball roommates by jumping up and down on their beds and zapping them with sparks from his bright orange tongue that crackled like lightning.

T-Tex3000 didn't jump up and down on Mighty Tighty Whitey, though. He lassoed him with his mechanical lasso instead. This made the hot-tempered underwear mad and he raced from room to room, towing T-Tex3000 like a water skier without the water. The little dinosaur slammed into walls, tables, and chairs until just about everything in the house was broken.

CHAPTER 2

Sidekicking and Screaming

A week ago (although it seemed like longer) Granny and I had taken in ten roommates to help pay the bills. We hadn't counted on ten lunatics—eleven if you count the two-headed baby as two. Yes, life had been insane at 1313 Thirteenth Street ever since the Super Goofballs moved in.

Also I had decided I was not going to be Granny's sidekick anymore. I was old enough to be my own superhero. So I needed a sidekick of my own, and my plan was to choose one of the Super Goofballs. But they were *such* goofballs.

Speaking of which, T-Tex3000 and Mighty Tighty Whitey burst into my room and leaped on top of me.

Dinosaur claws, no matter how small, do not feel good digging into your back. Wonder Boulder, Pooky the Paranormal Parakeet, SuperSass CuteGirl, the Impossibly Tough Two-Headed Infant (a.k.a., Biff and Smiff), and the Frankenstein Punster piled on two seconds later. We all ended up on the floor, tangled in Tex's lasso.

"I was going to choose one of you as a sidekick," I yelled, "but forget it!"

That got their attention.

They all really wanted the job.

"*I* can do it!"

"Choose me!"

"NO! ME, ME, ME, ME, ME!"

A super pillow fight broke out.

That woke Granny up. "Shine and rise!" she called, back-flipping out of bed and sliding backwards down the pole to the kitchen-lair. She is the Bodacious Backwards Woman. She says and does everything backwards. She whirled around the room in super-reverse—chopping, mixing, and frying—and three seconds later, screamed, *"Ready is breakfast!"*

Everything stopped, except the feathers floating in the air like slow-motion snowflakes. Stopping for food—anytime, anywhere—is the one thing all Super Goofballs can agree on. Still linked together by the lasso, we hopped through the hall, bounced down the stairs, and rolled to the breakfast table.

"Feed us! Feed us!" the roommates cried, opening their mouths like baby birds begging for worms. Funny thing: Pooky the Paranormal Parakeet actually *was* begging for worms. Granny tossed her a few to sprinkle on her pancakes.

"Yum!" chirped Pooky.

"That say you'd knew I!" said Granny. This was Pooky's favorite phrase and it cracked everyone up, especially the Impossibly Tough Two-headed Infant. Milk gushed out of Biff's nose and hit Smiff right in the eye. Food, of course, started flying.

I closed my TV screen, turned on the wipers, and watched the crazy show.

Hmmm. Which one of these loons would make the least horrible sidekick? It was a tough call. On a scale of one to ten, they were all at least twenty in horribleness.

CHAPTER 3
Emergency? What Emergency?

I had wrongly assumed that things would calm down a bit with Blunder Mutt out of the house (superbig enthusiasm + supertiny brain = lots and lots of super crashes and explosions). He and Super Vacation Man (huge, burly, Hawaiian shirt–wearing superguy with vacation-oriented superpowers, who dreams of one day actually taking a vacation) had teamed up the night before, when SVM got a phone call from Mayor What's-His-Name. Then they had raced off on an important assignment.

Blunder reminds SVM of his dear, departed dog, a tiny Shih Tzu named Scoodlyboot. Scoodlyboot ran away from home when Super Vacation Man was just Super Vacation *Toddler*. It haunts SVM to this day.

Super Vacation Man loves having another dog around, and Blunder Mutt believes he's "the grapest soup-ter hero in histree! I never ackshly seed him in his tree, but it musta bin a grape one!"

Blunder had actually been *my* sidekick for part of one day (that didn't work out very well), so as they took off, he apologized for leaving me: "I sorry, poor, saddy Mazy Tekko Doo. But it really fer the betters, 'cause if I be *your* sidekick, you be embarrassing by how super-dooper I is compareded to you."

Believe me, it was okay by me. Although I still needed a sidekick, Blunder Mutt definitely was not it. He was brave and he sure tried hard, but man, what a knucklehead. I'd constantly be

afraid of him accidentally blowing me up or something.

This new assignment must have been a dangerous and important one because Mayor What's-His-Name had been trying to reach Super Vacation Man all that day. I almost went along to help, but decided to let them handle it.

So now Super Vacation Man and Blunder Mutt were hang gliding across the sky, responding to a big emergency. Or so I thought. Of course, I wasn't there. There are things in this story that I didn't see with my own eyes. I had to put the whole story together later after talking to everyone involved.

For instance, I found out later that Super Vacation Man was just pretending to be responding to an emergency. He didn't even know there *was* a real emergency. Only Blunder Mutt knew. The mayor kept calling and getting Blunder on the phone. But when Blunder Mutt tried to pass on the message to Super Vacation Man and the rest of us, he was so Blunder Muttish that nobody believed or even understood him.

Later, when Super Vacation Man answered the phone, it was not the mayor calling. SVM pretended it was, but it was really a travel agent who had gotten him a room at the Hotel Le Grande, a beautiful tropical resort. Get it? It's kinda confusing. The mayor thought Super Vacation Man had gotten the message from Blunder. And Blunder thought he had given the message. And after Super Vacation Man got off the phone, we all thought they were leaving on an important mission.

But instead, Super Vacation Man was going on the first vacation of his life. He was thrilled.

He decided to pretend to be someone else. Because

HELP!

if people know you're a super-hero, your vacation is automatically ruined. They won't stop asking you to help them, even when they don't really *need* help:

"Super Vacation Man! Help me blow up my floatie!"

"Super Vacation Man! Help me put on my suntan lotion!"

"Super Vacation Man! Help me think of other things to ask you to help me with!"

And they don't even say please. Or thank you.

But he could never *not* help them, because he had taken an oath to always help out when called upon. It's in his super catchphrase. He even *promises*:

HELP!!!!

"Any time and any*where*,
call for help and I'll be there!
I promise!"

So he had to keep his superidentity quiet. He tried to explain it to Blunder Mutt.

"Listen, Blunder. We are going to use—*zip, bang*—phony names."

"Oh, goody, me love phoneys wiff names. I answer da phone named da Soupter Phone! I'm da Soupter Phone answerer!"

"No, Blunder. This has nothing to do with phones. I just don't want people to know who I am. It's called being incognito. You get it? In-cog-neeto."

"Neato!"

"Well, yes, I suppose it is neato, but the main thing is—*shh*—don't tell anyone my name. I'll be 'Mr. Smith' . . ."

"Then who will Mr. *Smith* be?"

"No, no. There *is* no Mr.

Smith. It's just a *phony* name."

"You so kookoo. A telephoney named Smith?"

"Okay, okay, Blunder, just listen: You'll be Mr. Jones. You won't be Blunder Mutt."

"How can me not be Blunder? Blunder is who me be!" He pointed to his face and then to his photo I.D. "See? . . . that *me!* Only teeny. And not movin' and talkin' so much!"

"Good point, Blunder. Now please stop talking so much."

"But Soupter, we need to talks about the importish mission we is on. I forgetted what the mayor say to me. What mission *is* we on?"

Now, Super Vacation Man is true blue. He prides himself on his honesty. He was already feeling guilty about pretending that he was going on a mission when he was actually going on vacation. But he told himself that that was just a small fib. And of course, as far as he knew, there *was* no emergency.

Now Blunder Mutt was asking him directly what they were flying off to do. Super Vacation Man *really* didn't want to lie. But he didn't want to admit to Blunder that he had already fibbed, so he fibbed again. Only he tried to do it without actually *saying* the fib.

"Blunder, have you ever heard of the Invisible Superbad Blue-Fanged Ferret?"

Super Vacation Man couldn't exactly remember who the Invisible Superbad Blue-Fanged Ferret was, but he knew he was famous. He couldn't remember if he was a supervillain or not. And he had no reason to think that the Ferret was within a thousand miles of where they were going, but still he wasn't *technically* lying.

"Ooooooh! A parrot that's bad *and* inbizzable?"

"Well, yes, but he's a *ferret*, not a *parrot*."

"How you know what he be if he be *inbizzable?*"

"You just know."

"Blue fangs, right?!"

"Right."

"How you *know* they blue?"

"You just know."

"But *how* you just know?"

"You. Just. Know. That's. How."

"Okay, I capture him!"

"If you'd like to, you could try to capture him."

"Like to? Yous kidding? I *loves* to capture him. But, but, but . . . if he inbizzable, how I *know* when I capture him?"

"I guess you just know that, too," said SVM.

"Soupy Vacater Man," said Blunder Mutt, "I soooo proud to get such a respoonsibiltity. All dogs be man's best friends, but I be *you's* bestest friend. I never let you down, ever, ever, ever. You know when I say, *'Whole wide worldy, hear me call . . . Blunder Nut be save you all'?* Well, *way* before I saves the whole wide worldy, I always will be savin' you first."

"That's great, Blunder," said Super Vacation Man. "And the same to you."

Super Vacation Man felt bad that he hadn't been totally truthful. But it was *possible* that the Invisible

Superbad Blue-Fanged Ferret was on vacation at the Hotel Le Grande. I mean, anything's *possible*, he said to himself. And while he was saying that to himself, most of his brain was dreaming about his dream vacation.

CHAPTER 4
The Big Contest

ack at the house, the phone rang for a long time before I remembered that Blunder Mutt was gone and no one else was going to answer it.

"House of Super Goofballs, Amazing Techno Dude speaking."

"Good morning, Mayor What's-His-Name speaking. And speaking of speaking, may I speak to Super Vacation Man?"

"He left hours ago."

"Hmmmm. That's funny. Actually, it's not funny. Completely unfunny. He was supposed to come to Gritty City City Hall, so I could tell him about an important case, and he hasn't shown up yet. I talked to that lunatic Blunder Mutt sixteen times. Did he give him the message?"

"Well, sort of. But you also talked to SVM on the phone last night, right?"

"Wrong."

"I was standing right next to him. He said, 'Hello, Mayor What's-His-Name! Yes, Mayor What's-His-Name! *Blam-bing-whammo*, Mayor What's-His-Name!"

"Well, maybe he was talking to some *other* Mayor What's-His-Name."

That seemed unlikely. Something was fishy here. Where the heck had SVM and Blunder Mutt gone? Were they okay?

"Frankly, my dude, I don't give a darn," said the mayor. "Tell you what. This was the perfect job for Super Vacation Man, but I'm calling on you to save the day instead. And the day is definitely in need of saving!"

"I'll be there in two seconds!"

"It can't wait that long. I'll tell you over the phone.

That supervillain sourpuss, Mondo Grumpo, is on the move, plotting something very grumpy."

"Sounds like a pain in the you-know-what, but grumpy is not exactly *evil*."

"This is no ordinary grumpiness! This is super*evil* grumpiness!"

"It can't be too evil. I've barely even *heard* of Mondo Grumpo. He's not even on the Slimy Sleazeball Superchart."

"Wrong. While you were busy sniffing out Queen Smellina the Shrieking Stinkbug of Stench, the rest of the evil world didn't just stop being evil, you know! Mondo Grumpo hit the superchart last week and moved up fast. In fact, he was number two until you threw Queen Smellina into jail. So, now he's . . ."

SLIMY SLEAZEBALL SUPER CHART

#1:

MONDO GRUMPO

#2

SUPER-SLUG ICKY INDIVIDUAL

"Number *one* on the Slimy Sleazeball Superchart?!"

"Wow, you are good at math. Anyway, Mondo Grumpo is anti-fun of any kind. He never laughs. Never smiles. His superpowers are super-grumpiness and negativity. He uses a superscolding technique called 'The Evil Finger Shake of Shame.' He shakes his finger and negative lightning bolts shoot from his fingertip. This, together with his horrifying, supergrumpy frown, delivers a deadly dose of disapproval. It makes his victims feel really, really bad. Even if you've done nothing wrong, you feel like your teacher has caught you cheating on a test . . . and you're in your underwear . . . and your underwear's full of holes . . . and the whole classroom, no, the whole *world*, is laughing at you. Only a million times worse. What would happen if he ever found out a way to do the Evil Finger Shake of Shame to the whole world?"

"Let me guess: every bit of fun in the world would be gone?"

"Wow, you are supersmart. I guess that's why you're a cool superdude."

"Being mayor is pretty cool, too."

"You think so? Today I have an all-day meeting with fifteen boring people making boring speeches. Every time I fall asleep, they poke me with pencils to wake me up and then start their boring speeches from the beginning again. You wanna trade places?"

"Well, no. I guess not."

"Okay, then, get going! Right away! Sooner if possible!"

"Are there any clues?" I asked.

"Last night my office window was broken by a huge, really nasty, moldy, supersour lemon," said Mayor What's-His-Name.

"That's funny," I said, "we got hit by a moldy lemon, too. At least one of us did."

"Follow the lemons," said the mayor.

CHAPTER 5

EXCUSE ME? VACATION?!

Of course, every goofball wanted to come along and be my sidekick. But I didn't have time to decide which one to take and there was no way I was taking *all* of them.

"Me, me, me, me!"

"No, me!"

Then I noticed a piece of paper on the kitchen counter. It was a to-do list written by Super Vacation Man.

Super Vacation Man had gone on vacation?

REMEMBER, FOR
THE MISSION:
★ 26 PAIRS of FLIP-FLOPS
(assorted colors)
★ 43 TUBES of SUNBLOCK
★ 4 AMUSING ANIMAL-
SHAPED INFLATABLE
FLOATIES. MAKE THAT 40.
★ GET READY FOR the BEST,
MAKE THAT THE FIRST
ZING! POW! ZOWEE!—
"MISSION" of this kind
EVER!!!
★ YIPPEEE!....

How could he go on vacation at a time like *this*?

Of course, I had no way of knowing that he didn't know about Mondo Grumpo. So I got mad.

But everyone else just got excited.

"*I* wanna go on vacation!"

"*Me!*"

"No, *meeeeeee!*"

"Nobody's going on vacation!" I said. "There are two parts to this mission. First, we need to find and battle that supervillain sourpuss, the diabolical

Mondo Grumpo. I'll do that. *Alone.* And second, *somebody* needs to find Super Vacation Man and Blunder Mutt, who seem to think that taking a vacation is more important than saving the world!"

"Me, me, me, me!"

"I . . . said . . . '*me*'!"

"No, *I* said 'me'!"

"You *all* said 'me'!" I said. "'*Me*' is all you ever say! But listen: me have . . . I mean *I* have an idea. You will *all* look for Super Vacation Man and Blunder Mutt. We'll make it a contest. The Super Goofball who finds those lazy bums will win—and the winner will be my sidekick."

They all screamed at the top of their lungs and ran toward the door, forgetting that it wasn't anywhere near big enough for that many superheroes to fit through at the same time. The whole doorframe got blown out. So there's one more thing I'll have to fix. But at least they were gone.

"All right, Granny, we're on our own on this one," I said.

But then a car horn tooted. Granny said that since we were no longer official partners, she had made other plans.

"Run to have I!" she said. Then she ran backwards toward the huge hole where the door used to be.

"Boyfriend new a have I." She giggled, diving backwards into a very fancy car.

The Bodacious Backwards Woman changes boyfriends like some people change socks.

"Well, then, can I borrow the keys to the Backwardsmobile?"

"Problemo no," she called. "Do I like just, carefully drive but!"

Drive carefully like her. Right. There are more dents in her car than stars in the universe.

CHAPTER 6

Action Packing

I rushed to the kitchen-lair and packed in superfast motion.

"Amazing Techno Dude Suitcase/Toolkit . . . check! Amazing Techno Handheld Remote (I had just rebuilt it and it was working better than ever) . . . check! Super-Chew Choco-Chunk Crusty-Crunch cookies . . . check!" Those were just to eat while pack-ing the other remaining items. "Check, check, check!" *Munch, munch, munch!*

The phone rang. It was the mayor again.

"You haven't left yet?"

"No, I had to pack!"

Actually, that's what I tried to say, but since I had eleven cookies in my mouth, it sounded more like, "Oh, ah hagga paff!"

I slammed the phone down. I hate impatient people. Except me. I like me.

I ran toward the door/hole.

Ring!

I ran back, still munching.

"Heffo!"

"I don't know what *you* said, but *I* said, 'You haven't left yet?!'"

"Ah leebing rye now!" Slam.

Ring!

"You're still there?!"

I swallowed the last crumb.

"I'm only here because someone keeps calling me!" I

slammed the phone down again. Some people can be so un-super sometimes.

The phone started ringing again, but I hopped into the Backwardsmobile, stomped on the gas pedal, and tore off backwards down the street in a cloud of blue smoke in search of Mondo Grumpo. And gigantic, moldy lemons.

CHAPTER 7
Hotel Le Grande

Meanwhile, Super Vacation Man and Blunder Mutt were landing on the beach at the Hotel Le Grande. Well, SVM landed on the beach and Blunder landed on a very large lady in a very small bikini who had been *sleeping* on the beach. Her screaming made all the other swimmers think a shark was attacking, which led to a whole lot more screaming. In the chaos, SVM and Blunder snuck away and into the hotel's superfancy lobby, which was packed with families on vacation.

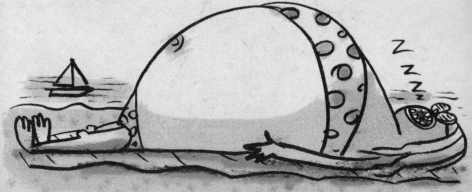

DING!
DING!
DING!

Super Vacation Man and Blunder Mutt approached the front desk.

SVM was excited to finally be on a real vacation. "Okay, Blunder, just be quiet and let me do the talking,"

"Hello, madame," said SVM to the woman behind the desk. "I'm Mr. Smith and this is Mr. Jones. We have reservations for two—*zip! kapow! phhht! ding-dang-dong!*—superdeluxe rooms!"

"Okay . . ." said the woman suspiciously, "but what on earth were those noises?"

"What noises?" said Super Vacation Man. "I didn't hear any noises."

"Those loud, obnoxious noises that just came out of your mouth," she said. "Who are you *really*?"

"Why, we're nobody in particular," said Super Vacation Man. "Just a couple of normal, un-super nobodies on vacation!"

This got the attention of Mr. Spaulding Spittleman, the hotel manager.

He had a huge, friendly grin on his face, but every-thing he said was nasty. And he spit when he talked.

"Did s-s-someone s-s-say nobodies-s-s?" spit Spittleman.

"That's be us!" said Blunder Mutt.

Spittleman looked through his reservation book.

"Oh, yes, I s-seeeee now." He spit again. "We have *plenty* of room-s-s. Just none for nobodies-s-s-s." That last one was a big spit.

Blunder was confused.

"I cornfused!" he said.

"I'm confused, too," said Spittleman. "Confused about why you're s-s-s-still s-s-s-s-standing there!"

"Well, *my* cornfusedness," said Blunder, "is 'cause you be looking so way nicer than you speaks! Show some respectacles! Dis fakey Smith is really the *really* SOUPY VACATIONER MAN! And me his sidekicker!" And then he whispered, "But, shush! We traveling *in* dog neato!"

"S-s-s-super Vacation Man?" said Spittleman.

"Why didn't you s-s-say s-s-so?"

Spaulding Spittleman probably would have figured it out anyway—Super Vacation Man looked so darn super and all—but SVM couldn't believe that Blunder blew his cover.

"I don't want to hear another word out of you!" SVM shouted.

"How 'bout a whole buncha words?" asked Blunder.

"That's not funny!" said Super Vacation Man.

But Blunder wasn't trying to be funny.

Spittleman said that of course he had a room for Super Vacation Man. A short, grunting, drooling, bearded woman—Madame Zombina the Bellhop— helped with his luggage and showed him to his room.

SVM tried to strike up a conversation. "So . . . how long have you been a bellhop?"

"*Grunt, grunt, drool, drool,*" she replied.

"How wonderful for you," said Super Vacation Man.

But things weren't so wonderful for Blunder Mutt. That "in dog neato" line tipped off Spittleman to the fact that Blunder Mutt was actually a dog. Since dogs were not allowed in the hotel, he threw Blunder out the door,  cheerfully calling, "Have a nice trip, and I *won't* s-s-see you next fall, you s-s-stupid, s-s-stinking s-s-spaniel!" (Blunder's not a spaniel. Spittleman chose that word for its excellent spit-ability.)

Blunder returned ten seconds later in disguise. He was wearing a small palm tree from the front lawn. Spittleman pretended not to know it was Blunder Mutt and cheerfully ordered Madame Zombina the Bellhop to plant the runaway palm in a flowerpot in the lobby. Then Spittleman commanded the palm tree to "*stay!*"

CHAPTER 8
Globetrotting Goofballs

Meanwhile, the roommates were crisscrossing the globe, looking for Super Vacation Man and Blunder Mutt. They caused chaos wherever they went.

The Impossibly Tough Two-headed Infant started a riot in Mexico City when Biff and Smiff started fighting over a bean burrito in a crowded restaurant.

SuperSass CuteGirl caused a scandal when she met the Queen of England and said: "You are in desperate need of a super makeover, Your Royal Frumpiness." A department store in India was closed down indefinitely after some guy mistook Mighty Tighty Whitey for a regular pair of underpants and tried to try him on.

So, although the goofballs were searching for clues all over the world, they were finding only trouble.

CHAPTER 9
The "H" Word

Back at the hotel, Super Vacation Man wanted to start his fabulous vacation. Unfortunately, his room was a disaster area: filthy bathroom, exploding TV, no mint on the pillow. And hot! It was like 200 degrees in there. The A/C had gone haywire. The controls were stuck on "Blasting, Scorching, Hot, Hot, Heat."

SVM called the front desk and asked for help.

Mr. Spaulding Spittleman arrived at the door, smiled wide, and spit out, "I'm afraid our maid is out s-s-s-sick. But s-s-since you're s-s-so darn *s-s-super*, *S-S-Super Vacation Man*, we would be deeply honored if *you* would help *us* ins-s-s-s-stead!"

Oh, boy . . . here we go. Super Vacation Man must help those in need, even hotel managers with bad attitudes.

"S-s-so," spit Spittleman. "Guess-s-s who's-s-s on duty?"

"The only thing I'm *on* is *vacation!*" he cried, covering his ears.

But Spittleman asked again, this time more loudly: "Pleas-s-se S-S-Super Vacation Man, pleas-s-se *help!*"

That was it. Super Vacation Man couldn't say no.

Madame Zombina the Bellhop handed him a cleaning lady uniform. Super Vacation Man

sighed, put on the protective facemask, rubber gloves, and frilly apron, and sadly said, "Any time and anywhere, call for help and I'll be there. I . . . promise."

"Mos-s-st exc-c-c-cellent," spit Spaulding Spittleman.

CHAPTER 10
Backwards Blastoff

eanwhile, cruising backwards along the highway at 611 miles per hour, I used my TV Helmet satellite tracking system to follow the scent of moldy lemons.

I lost the trail for a minute, but after a few tweaks in the citrus-tracking system, my computer was able to fill in the gaps of the lemon path and determine its exact point of origin.

"Let's see . . . it seems to be coming from a coastal region, a resort area of some kind . . . aha! The Hotel Le Grande!" I cried, but then screeched to a halt. I was stuck in bumper-to-bumper traffic.

I opened my suitcase/toolkit and made some small improvements on Granny's old car. Well, maybe not that small. When I finished, I pressed the new blast-off button on the dashboard and the Backwardsmobile tipped up on its rear wheels (really the front wheels) and shot skyward, in what was now the Backwardsrocketmobile. I'd be at the hotel in no time.

CHAPTER 11

The Invisible Ferret

ack in the hotel lobby, Blunder was battling a swarm of tiny bugs that lived in the palm tree he was wearing. The bugs were so tiny they were almost invisible. Blunder believed he was under attack by the Invisible Superbad Blue-Fanged Ferret.

"You don't know who you be messing with, you inbissible fangy parrot, you!"

He started hopping around the lobby, karate-chopping the air.

The hotel guests noticed this strange behavior.

"Gee, Billy," said a dad, "that tree is a pretty good dancer."

"For a tree," said Billy.

CHAPTER 12
super scrubbing Man

Super Vacation Man was working hard: making beds, cleaning bathrooms, putting those paper strips on the toilet seats . . . It was way worse than being at home, where, I can tell you, he never did any chores.

He kept trying to sneak away to have fun. He signed up for all kinds of activities, but his cleaning duties got in the way. He even tried using one of his superpowers, Super Time-sharing, so that he could be in two places at once. While one of him was scraping an old, dried, gross, green, sticky milkshake from a room's ceiling, the other snuck off to play a little badminton. Things were going well for a serve or two until Mr. Spaulding Spittleman spotted him and put the second him to work scrubbing badminton shoes with a toothbrush. Super Time-sharing meant twice the misery.

"It is s-s-such a great honor to have you s-s-super-s-s-slaving away like this-s-s," spit Spittleman.

Super Vacation Man was also getting worried about Blunder Mutt. Where was he? He was sorry he'd gotten angry with him. He also felt very bad about the fibbing. And about that whole ferret thing. He was afraid that Blunder had run away just like Scoodlyboot did so many years ago. He tried calling for Blunder Mutt.

"Blunder . . . Mutt . . . where—*zip, whoosh, bye-bye*—arrrrre youuuuuu?"

BLUNDER MUTT!!

CHAPTER 13
On the trail of the
invisible ferret or parrot

B lunder heard him, but didn't answer. Super Vacation Man had said that he didn't want to hear another word out of him. So Blunder decided to just be quiet. He can be very obedient, especially when you don't want him to be.

Besides, he was hard at work on his mission! His karate chopping had scared away the bugs and *he* thought he'd scared away the Invisible Superbad

Blue-Fanged Ferret.

"You can run, invibsible parrot," he said, "but you can't hide from this patickullar Mutt of Blunder!"

He had to go find him! But there was one problem: He'd been told to "stay" by that terrible Spaulding Spittleman. Although it was difficult for a good dog such as himself to disobey a "stay" command, in the end he decided that saving the world from a superbad invisible parrot was more important than obeying a rude hotel manager. He pushed his legs through the bottom of the pot and started racing around the hotel.

So now this insane palm tree was spying on all the guests, tiptoeing here and there, bumping into things, breaking into rooms—on the trail of an invisible ferret, who he thought was a parrot, who in reality wasn't even in the same time zone.

Blunder was serious about his snooping and took notes wherever he went. He spelled every word out loud as he wrote.

"Where . . . w-a-i-r . . . is . . . i-z . . . inbissible . . . n-b-z-b-l-l-l-l . . . parrot . . . p-e-a-r . . . i-t?"

"Gosh, Sally, that tree is spelling something," said a guest.

"Dad, that tree is a very bad speller."

Super Vacation Man ran by, pushing a cartful of mops and brooms, but Blunder didn't recognize him in his cleaning lady uniform.

"Gee, they sure grow washer ladies biggish and strongish round here," he whispered.

CHAPTER 14
The Grumpy Mad Scientist's Laboratory

While Super Vacation Man ran around cleaning and looking for Blunder Mutt, and Blunder ran around looking for invisible parrots, something much more sinister was going on in the hotel.

Mr. Spaulding Spittleman and Madame Zombina the Bellhop entered the hotel elevator. Madame Zombina carried a large, glowing, moldy, yellow-green suitcase. Spittleman took out a special moldy, yellow-green key from his pocket and inserted it into a keyhole near the elevator buttons. The elevator filled with moldy, yellow-

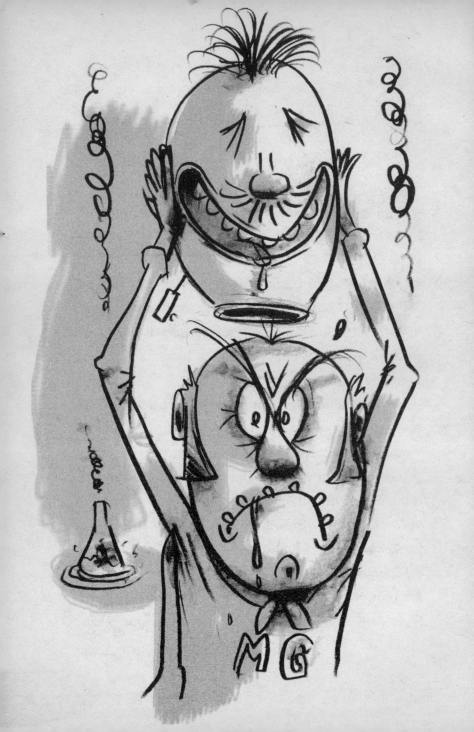

green light and it shot down fast, past the basement to the secret subbasement. Maybe even the sub-subbasement. It was way down there.

The doors opened and they stepped into a very large room. Moldy, yellow-green flames under bottles of bubbling, moldy, yellow-green liquids made clouds of moldy, yellow-green steam and smoke. Obviously a secret laboratory. Obviously moldy and lemony. Obviously evil.

Then Spittleman put his hands on either side of his face and lifted his head up off his shoulders.

He took his head off. Ahhhhhh! Spittleman took his head off! And the head was still smiling.

No, wait, it was a fake head! There was another head underneath. He handed his fake, smiling head to Madame Bellhop, who hung it on the fake, smiling head rack.

The real face underneath wasn't smiling. Far from it. There has never been a more unsmiling face. It was the kind of face you look at and it makes you afraid to breathe. It's something about the superfreaky frown. And the disgusting, moldy, yellow-green teeth dripping with disgusting, moldy, yellow-green liquid something. And the glowing, squinting, supermean eyes staring back at you with such meanness it stings your eyes and then keeps stinging through the back of your eyes to your brain.

This face could only belong to one horrible supervillain: Mondo Grumpo.

He stood there and frowned for a minute. Then he snapped his fingers and sneered in the grumpiest voice ever: "SOUR ME UP!"

Madame Zombina the Bellhop opened the suitcase. Inside were perfect rows of gigantic, glowing, moldy, supersour lemons. And I mean *super*sour. They made people's eyes water and sting on the other side of town. Madame Zombina tossed one to Mondo Grumpo and he ate it like an apple. As soon as he finished that one, he snapped his fingers again and Madame Zombina instantly flipped him another, which he spun like a small basketball on his finger and then ate in a flurry of chomps.

Mondo Grumpo had developed these horrible lemons in his secret laboratory. They helped him maintain his famous frown. His fingers were moldy and yellow-green, and so were his eyes. He was sweating moldy, yellow-green sweat.

"You know, Madame Zombina." Mondo Grumpo frowned. "I'd be smiling and laughing really hard right now if I didn't really hate smiling and laughing."

Madame Zombina the Bellhop just grunted and drooled.

Mondo continued. "Ruining Super Vacation Man's vacation is like a fantastic vacation for me! Making him miserable is exactly the kind of thing that makes being an evil, ugly, grumpy supervillain worthwhile. It does my evil, moldy heart good. Can you believe he fell for that phony phone call? When I pretended to be that stupid travel agent? I mean, if I were a laugher, I'd sure be laughing about that!"

Madame Zombina grunted

and drooled some more.

"And this is just a warm-up for my bigger, eviler plan: 'The Death of Fun'! I will ruin the vacations of every man, woman, and child staying at this hotel! I'll convert this resort into a place of pure misery! And this is only one of a *chain* of hotels. All the Hotel Le Grandes will now be Hotel Le Grims! Yes! Yes! I would so love to laugh one of those supervillain evil laughs right about now, except, you know, I don't *do* that!"

Just then, the elevator doors opened and out jumped a palm tree.

CHAPTER 15

the evil finger shake of shame

"**G**otcha, you dumb-dumb head!" said our favorite very brave, very dumb dog. "You is not so invibisal as you think! And, wowser, you is the biggestest parrot I ever seed. Plus, where the hecksh is your feathers and beaks?"

Mondo Grumpo had absolutely no idea what Blunder was talking about. He just took him prisoner. Madame Zombina tied him up.

Blunder just laughed.

"I reporty you both to Spauldy Spootlemam, the hotel mammager!"

Grumpo laughed, too, but then stopped himself, remembering that he *never* laughs. "My dear, dumb palm tree dog. The Spittleman you are thinking of was *me* wearing a fake head! The *real* Spittleman is away on a trip!"

This concept was far beyond Blunder Mutt. He looked at Grumpo like he was an idiot.

"You poor grumpy dodo head. You jess don't gets it, does you? Muss be hardish to be so stoopish. Kinda saddish. I . . . speak . . . slowier: I . . . gonna . . . reporty . . . you . . . to . . . Spauldy . . . Spootle . . . mam. The . . . mam . . . ma . . . ger. Yer teenyish brainy understab now?"

Mondo Grumpo lost it. He yelled so loud, some of the bottles of bubbling moldy, yellow-green liquids exploded.

"UNDERSTAND? THERE IS NOTHING *TO* UNDERSTAND, EXCEPT THAT YOU ARE THE DUMBEST DUMB DOG IN DUMB DOG HISTORY!"

This scared the heck out of Blunder Mutt. He put his tail between his legs and got down low to the ground.

"I ORDER YOU TO WHIMPER!" said Mondo Grumpo.

"Wimpo?" said Blunder in a small, sad voice.

Blunder was now suffering from the dreaded Bad Dog Syndrome. This is not what happens when dogs really *are* bad; it's when they *think* they're bad.

Grumpo had him where he wanted him. It was time for the Evil Finger Shake of Shame. He shook his finger violently, sending moldy, yellow-green, negative lightning bolts right into Blunder's eyes.

"THE EVIL FINGER
    MAKES YOU SHIVER;
YOUR SWEAT AND
    TEARS RUN LIKE A
    RIVER;
YOU FEEL BAD
    RIGHT DOWN TO
    YOUR LIVER . . .
BAD, BAD DOG!!!"

Blunder felt afraid.

He felt ashamed.

And finally, he just felt really, really bad.

Mondo Grumpo melted Blunder Mutt into a puddle on the floor. It was like a candle or a wicked witch melting or something.

And then, Mondo Grumpo, using his bare hands, like some kind of psycho-sculptor, reformed Blunder Mutt. He pushed and smooshed his face and body around like he was working in clay.

"There, you idiotic mutt," grumbled Mondo, "that's much better. You are now a Nincompoop of Numbness!"

The new Blunder had a very distant look in his eyes. He had a huge frown on his face. He had always been such an excited, happy guy, but now he just drooled. And grunted. Here's what he grunted:

"Life stinkish. I stinkish. Everything be stinkish. Me no care 'bout nuthin'."

"Excellent," Grumpo continued. "Now say hello to another of my nice, numb nincompoops: Madame Zombina the Bellhop."

Blunder and Madame Zombina looked at each other. Actually, they were so numb, you couldn't tell if they were really *seeing* each other. But they did say hello. Sort of.

"*Grunt, drool*, who cares," grunted Madame Zombina.

"*Drool, grunt*, me no care 'bout nuthin'," grunted Blunder Mutt.

CHAPTER 16

SKIPPY THE TV REPAIR BOY

t that exact second, I came screaming out of the sky in the Backwardsrocketmobile and arrived with a crash on the beach at the

Hotel Le Grande. I landed right on the picnic lunch of a very large woman in a very small bikini. She screamed, "Not again! Huge men, crazy dogs, and now boys with TV heads?"

I had no idea what she was talking about. Remember, I had no idea that Super Vacation Man or Blunder Mutt were at this hotel.

Something was stinging my eyes and making them cry like rivers. Then I noticed a moldy-lemony haze in the air. It was coming from a trail of chewed-up, moldy lemon peels that led right to the front door of the hotel.

But wait. I'm a pretty famous superhero and Mondo Grumpo might recognize me. I ducked behind a hedge to think about how to disguise my identity. Then I noticed a poster in front of the hotel. It was advertising a character appearing as part of a National TV Repairman Convention.

I looked at the photo of the character. He was called Skippy the TV Repair Boy. And the funny thing was, he *also* had a TV head! In fact, he looked a lot like me, except he had a big, bushy beard. At first I was angry that someone was copying my look, but then I had an idea. I could pretend to be Skippy the TV Repair Boy!

I quickly removed a bad toupee from a rich-looking fellow and attached it to my chin.

I walked right in through the lobby and up to the front desk.

"Skippy the TV Repair Boy, reporting for duty!" I said cheerfully, stroking my beard.

"Oh, thank goodness, you made it!" said the woman behind the counter. "Here's your key—Room 207. Go get settled and hurry to the convention hall!

Nice beard, by the way."

I ran down the hall and took the stairs to the second floor. I opened the door to Room 207 and couldn't believe my eyes. The room was a total wreck. Dirty under-wear, soda bottles, and half-eaten pizza slices all over the floor. It reminded me of home—and not in a good way.

I called the front desk.

"This is Skippy the TV Repair Boy and my room is a pigsty!"

"Terribly sorry," said the voice on the phone, "we'll take care of it right away!"

"Thanks! That's what I call service!"

But then I waited and waited and waited.

And waited some more.

I called again: "Hello! This is Skippy the TV Repair Boy again! My room is still a pigsty!"

"Terribly sorry, we'll take care of it right away."

"That's what you said twenty minutes ago!"

CHAPTER 17
Goofballs Incoming!

The other Super Goofballs had been racing all over the world, getting into trouble, looking for Super Vacation Man and Blunder Mutt. Finally their search led them all to the same place—the Hotel Le Grande. They'd looked everywhere else in the world, and this was in fact the very last place *to* look. They were all running, flying, leaping, and bouncing toward the exact same spot—the middle of the hotel lobby—at the exact same moment.

Mighty Tighty Whitey, Pooky the Paranormal Parakeet, SuperSass CuteGirl, the Impossibly Tough Two-Headed Infant, Wonder Boulder, the Frankenstein Punster, and T-Tex3000 all shouted the things they shout when they arrive somewhere.

SuperSass: "Super sassiness—incoming!"

Mighty Tighty Whitey: "Super undies—incoming!"

Wonder Boulder: "Look out, everybody—this gonna hurt!"

They all crashed into each other and were knocked out cold. Except for Wonder Boulder, who crashed through the floor, crawled back out, and fainted.

They'd been on a long journey. They were sweaty, dirty, and now, unconscious. They didn't look very super.

Madame Zombina the Bellhop and a certain palm tree/dog stared at the pile of Super Goofballs, who didn't look at all like guests in a fancy hotel. Blunder was too numb to recognize them. Bellhop and palm tree/dog looked at each other. They grunted and drooled and then dragged all the goofballs out behind the hotel and tossed them into a very large trashcan.

Two seconds later a gigantic cleaning lady threw a bucket of dirty, soapy water out of a fifth-story window, right into that same trashcan. This woke the Super Goofs.

"I predict that that odd bellhop and palm tree will not let us back into that hotel," said Pooky the Paranormal Parakeet.

"Brilliant prediction," said Mighty Tighty Whitey.

Just then, a large TV-shaped van pulled up and out popped the *real* Skippy the TV Repair Boy, who ran right into the lobby. Madame Zombina and the palm tree waved him in.

SuperSass CuteGirl squealed, but in a whispery way: "Like, I've got a great idea!"

All the other Super Goofballs looked at her.

"I think a great idea . . ." said Biff.

" . . . sounds like a great idea right about now," said Smiff.

"A *smashing* idea," said Mighty Tighty Whitey.

"Me *love* smashing ideas," said Wonder Boulder.

"HEY, PUNS MY DEPARTMENT," said the Frankenstein Punster.

"Like, okay," said SuperSass,

"Here it is: *Let's go shopping!*"

She jumped out and ran down the street toward a mall. All the other goofball roommates chased after her, yelling things like, *"Shopping?"*, *"Did she say shopping?"*, and *"Come back here, you spoiled brat—this is no time for shopping!"*

CHAPTER 18
ONE EXTRA-LARGE CLEANING LADY

eanwhile, I was still waiting for someone to come and clean my room. This was getting ridiculous! I had a world to save! But I wasn't backing down.

"This is Skippy the TV Repair Boy and this room is a—"

"Terribly sorry, we'll take care of that right away."

"But that's what you—"

"Terribly sorry, we'll take care of that right away."

"Do you ever say anything besides—"

"Terribly sorry, we'll take care of that right away."

I finally realized I was talking to a recording.

I slammed the phone down and went out into the hallway.

A large, muscular cleaning lady was pushing her cart out of another room down at the end. She had a protective facemask, huge, hairy arms and legs, and a cleaning lady apron that was too small for her.

"Excuse me, miss," I called, "I'm Skippy the TV Repair Boy, kind of a celebrity here in the hotel. This disgusting room needs to be cleaned. Maybe some sweeping, scrubbing, and mopping?"

"*Oh, you think maybe some sweeping, scrubbing, and mopping?*" she yelled back. She had the deepest, loudest, and angriest voice of any cleaning lady I'd ever met. "*Aren't you forgetting something, Skippy?!*"

"Hmmm . . . now that you mention it," I said, "a little window washing would be nice."

The large cleaning lady blew a large fuse.

"*No, Skippy, a little win-*

dow washing definitely would not be nice! No, what you forgot is you forgot to say please!! I work my fingers to the bone and none of you people ever say please! Or thank you either, thank you very much! And mean-while—helloooo—I am sup-posed to be on—zip, zowee, yippee—vacation!!!"

That last part rang a bell. Did I *know* this lady? But I had no time to think about it, because she was running right at me. In one hand she was holding six or seven brooms and mops like spears. In the other was a huge spray bottle of industrial-strength toilet cleaning liquid, which she was aiming at me like a huge water gun. The closer she got, the bigger she looked. And she had looked pretty big from far away. This was one terrifying cleaning lady.

I ran back into the room and slammed the door. But she crashed right through it.

This was crazy! Here I was, on the trail of Mondo Grumpo, number one on the Slimy Sleazeball

Superchart, and I was doing battle with a crazy cleaning lady!

"Listen, ma'am," I pleaded, "I'm really sorry about this. I really should have said please, so I'm saying it now: Please! And here're some thank-yous in advance: Thank you, thank you, thank you!"

"Too little, too late, Skippy!"

She squirted a mighty blast of toilet cleaner in my face. Luckily, my monitor screen was closed.

"Wait!" I cried, opening the screen to get a better look.

Next came two

ARRRR-
GOWWW-
EEEE-
ACK-
ACK
ACK!

or three bucket-fuls of hot, soapy water.

"Blub, blub, blub!" I blubbed.

She yelled a yell that sounded more like a prehistoric animal than a human employed in the cleaning industry:

"ARRRRRRRRR-GOWWWWW-EEEEE-ACK-ACK-ACK!"

I looked at her wild, angry face, half covered by the facemask. I'd never seen a lady with a chin that big. Her adam's apple was bigger than a *real* apple. Her five o'clock shadow was more like a *midnight* shadow. Her forearms were like four*teen* arms. Okay, you get the picture: she was big. And she looked so familiar. But I knew there was no way I'd ever met this gigan-tic mop-chucker before. If I had, I would never have forgotten it.

Then she stretched her arms and faked a yawn. "Gee, Skippy, I'm feeling a little sweepy. It must be sweepy time!"

She heaved four brooms at me, like she was throwing darts—*thwwwt! thwwwt! thwwwt! thwwwt!*—and they pierced my clothing and pinned me to the closet door. I mean, broom handles aren't even sharp—that's how hard she threw them. I couldn't move.

Then she whipped out a toilet plunger and shmooshed it onto my face.

"*Time to*—push, pull, push, pull—*take the plunge!*" she said.

I reached for my Amazing Techno Dude Handheld Remote. Of course it wasn't in its holster.

It hardly ever is, even though I am positive I'd put it there before I'd left home. It also wasn't in my front or back pockets. Where was it? What the heck *is* it with remotes?

She pulled the plunger off of my face. It made a hollow suction-popping sound—and it really cleared my sinuses, by the way. Before she plunged again, I ripped my shirt, dove out of the way, and rolled into the hallway. This maid must be reported to the management!

Meanwhile, she replunged, missed me, and crashed through the closet door, through the wall, and into the hallway, right behind me.

CHAPTER 19

The Battle Rages On

e crashed through walls, windows, and into fountains. Mops, rags, and bursting bottles of cleaning fluids flew. We bounced through guest rooms, across the lawn, down the beach, and onto the hotel roof. Then we crashed through a huge skylight and into the hotel lobby.

The lobby looked different than it had an hour ago. It seemed drabber, duller, and moldier. More depressing. The signs that used to say "Hotel Le Grande" now said "Hotel Le Grim." The huge room was full of guests, but they didn't even react. It was like it was no big thing to see a TV-headed superhero crashing through the ceiling with a pumped-up cleaning lady maniac.

They were all like zombies! What the heck was wrong with them?

Mops, rags, and bursting bottles of cleaning fluids bounced off me, exploding everywhere, turning the lobby into a clean, but dangerous, war zone. Even sponges became weapons! How could someone hurt you with a sponge? Turns out if a sponge is soaked in toxic cleaning liquids and thrown at two or three hundred miles an hour, it can really sting. I was in danger of being air-freshened and disinfected to death!

"Take that, you crummy hotel guest!" the cleaning lady yelled. *"You are all the same . . . 'I need this! I need that! More pillows! More towels! More tiny bottles of shampoo!' Well, this cleaning lady needs something, too! I need a vacation!"*

"Okay, forget it!" I yelled back. "Go on vacation! Don't worry about me! As far as I'm concerned, you can hang up your mop forever! I can live with a little dirt!"

But she wouldn't listen.

She jumped on a huge floor buffer, yanked the starter cord, and revved it up. The machine roared, spewing a huge cloud of black smoke. She was riding it like a motorcycle or a jet ski or a snowmobile or something.

"Prepare to be rubbed out!" she screamed, and took off toward me.

CHAPTER 20
This kinda Rubs Me the wrong way

Where the heck was the remote? I looked again in all the places I'd looked before: holster, front pockets, back pockets . . . where was it? The floor buffer was so loud it was hard to think.

Then I realized I had forgotten something about remotes: the best way to find one is to not look for it. And that's what I did.

The crazy cleaning lady flew toward me, the floor buffer roaring like some kind of mechanical monster.

I held out my hand and closed my eyes. I pressed down hard with my thumb, as if I were holding a remote and pressing Pause. Then I opened my eyes.

I don't know where it came from, but there the

remote was, in
the palm of my hand. I looked
up. About ten feet above me, the
floor buffer and the huge, angry
cleaning lady had paused in midair.
Her face was frozen in an expression I'd
have to describe as beyond freaky . . . yet
familiar.

Then the cleaning lady uniform, finally stretched to its
limit, fell in tatters to the floor.
(But don't worry, those weren't
the only clothes she had on. She
was also wearing a Super Vacation
Man outfit.)

A Super Vacation Man outfit?

Wait a minute. No *wonder* she looked so familiar.

I looked up at Super Vacation Man in disbelief. How did he end up at this hotel? Was he on the mission to find Mondo Grumpo after all? And why the heck was he dressed like a cleaning lady?

"Super Vacation Man! It's me, Amazing Techno Dude!" I was still pretty mad at him. "How could you just run off on vacation? And why the heck are you using a vacation to work as a cleaning lady? And where's Blunder Mutt? And what are you doing here? *I'm* here to track down a supervillain named Mondo Grumpo!"

And then the Pause wore off. Super Vacation Man had just enough time to say, "Amazing Techno Dude?!"—

before he and the floor buffer fell toward me.

I quickly aimed the remote and pressed Rewind. Unfortunately, I missed the Rewind button and hit Fast Forward instead. Super Vacation Man and the huge floor buffer crashed on top of me with exactly forty-two times the force of gravity.

Which hurt.

My remote smashed into a million pieces.

The floor buffer buffed us but good. Then it took off down a hallway with a roar.

I lay there with Super Vacation Man, both of us squashed like bugs.

What happened? It made no sense. How had we both arrived at the same hotel? Where was Blunder Mutt? Where was Mondo Grumpo? Was all this part of his evil plot? What the heck was going on?

CHAPTER 21
Enter the Grumpmeister

The elevator bell went *ding!* and the doors opened. A potted palm tree and a bearded lady bellhop pushed out a fancy, moldy, golden green luggage cart full of glowing, moldy, yellow-green suitcases.

I looked closer and was amazed to see that the palm tree was actually Blunder Mutt. But his eyes looked dead. He was drooling and grunting. Blunder Mutt, usually so wild, so free, so wonderfully idiotic—what had happened to him?

"Well, well, well," growled someone in a very grumpy voice. "If it isn't Amazing Twerpy Dude."

I looked up. At the very top of the moldy suitcases sat a very scary-looking someone with a superfreaky frown. He had moldy, yellow-green teeth dripping with moldy, yellow-green something. And super-mean eyes that stared at me with such meanness it stung my eyes and kept stinging through the back of my eyes to my brain. It was absolutely, completely, totally impossible not to know who this was.

"And who might you be?" I said. "Because I don't keep track of the lesser-known, low-level supervillains."

"Lesser known?" he squawked. "I just so happen to be number one on the Slimy Sleazeball Superchart!"

"Wow, they're really lowering their standards," I said.

"Lowering their standards? I'm the one, the only, the supernegative living legend of evil, evil grumpiness—Mondo Grumpo!"

"You don't say," I said.

"I *do* say. And you know what the headline in tomorrow's *Gritty City Times* will say?" growled

Mondo Grumpo. "'Amazing Techno Dude and Super Vacation Man Squashed Like Bugs by Big Bad Buffer.' If I believed in funniness, I might find that funny."

"I find *you* funny," I said.

"NO, YOU DON'T!" he said. "BECAUSE I'M *NOT* FUNNY! DON'T YOU *DARE* CALL ME FUNNY!"

"Okay, Mr. Funny," I said.

"STOP THAT!" he said.

"Mr. Sillybilly. Joe Giggles. Mondo Funny-O."

"STOP, STOP, STOP!!!"

A few sharp giggles escaped from Mondo Grumpo's mouth, but he slapped himself and snapped his fingers five times. The lady bellhop opened one of the glowing, moldy, yellow-green suitcases and tossed him five moldy, supersour lemons.

Mondo spun them on his fingertips, and then quickly gobbled them up, sending moldy, supersour lemon peels and juice flying. This Mondo guy was really into lemons. And he was seriously nutso.

CHAPTER 22

The Chandelier of Nincompoopism

 ondo's frown deepened. It seemed as if the corners of his mouth might actually go past his jawline and off his face.

"You know, it was no accident that you and Super Vacation Man ended up here," he said. "You are both important parts of my evil plan."

He turned to Blunder and the bearded lady bellhop.

"Madame Zombina and bad, stupid dog/tree: PREPARE THE CHANDELIER OF NINCOM-POOPISM!"

Madame Zombina drooled and grunted: "*Drool, grunt,* whatever."

Blunder Mutt replied, "*Grunt, drool,* me still no care 'bout nuthin'."

Zombina and Blunder walked over to the wall and untied a rope fastened there. Letting it slide through their fingers, they lowered a huge, fancy light fixture to the floor.

They bound Super Vacation Man and me to the chandelier with chains. We were still too squished by the buffer to fight back. Then they pulled on the rope, lifting us high above the crowd. I recognized those chains: 100% Guaranteed Superhero Proof. I'd seen an ad for them in the *Super Globe Gazette*.

Super Vacation Man looked down at Blunder, standing there wearing the palm tree with that dead-eye stare, drooling. He had shed most of his leaves. His face was covered with dirt. The bugs had returned and were buzzing around his face. He was a poor excuse for a superhero, or even a palm tree. And he was totally under the control of Mondo Grumpo.

"I can't believe I've lost another—*woof, bark, ruff-ruff*—dog!" cried Super Vacation Man. He, of course, felt extra terrible, because this all reminded him of how he'd lost Scoodlyboot years ago. "Oh, Blunder," cried Super Vacation Man, "do you know how very, very—*sob, gush, honk*—sorry I am that I fibbed and then yelled at you?"

But Blunder Mutt was way too out of it to hear this apology. He just drooled and grunted some more: "Me no know nuthin'."

"You evil, grumpy maniac," I yelled at Mondo Grumpo. "What have you done to Blunder Mutt?"

"Yes," said Super Vacation Man, "what have you . . ." His voice trailed off. He looked angry, then sad, then far, far away.

He was squinting and staring

at Mondo Grumpo.

"Mr. Grumpo," he whispered, "you look very, very . . ."—he paused so long, I thought he fell asleep—"*familiar.*"

He was remembering a day back when he was Super Vacation Toddler.

He was running in slow motion through beautiful green grass with Scoodlyboot, his tiny dog. They were superhappy about how they were going on vacation together and how incredibly fun it was going to be! All of a sudden, an awful, frowning bully sped by on a bike, snatched Scoodlyboot, and rode off! "NO!" cried Super Vacation Toddler, "bring back my Scoodlyboot!"

CHAPTER 23

OLD ENEMIES

Super Vacation Man woke from his daydream.

"Now I remember!" he yelled, pointing at the supervillain. "Scoodlyboot didn't run away! *You stole her, Mondo Grumpo! Plus you ruined that vacation! Just like you're ruining this one!*"

"Oops, you got me there," said Mondo Grumpo, as if he didn't care at all.

But he did care. He hated Super Vacation Man. Boy, did he hate him. He hated his ability to have fun. He hated his vacation powers. He hated his smile, his laugh, everything. He'd

hated him when
they were kids, and
his hate had gotten
stronger and stronger over
the years. He was staring at him with
a stare that said all that.

Super Vacation Man didn't notice. Now he
was looking at the drooling lady bellhop.

"And you, lady bellhop," he said, "there's
something awfully familiar about *you*, too. That
nose, that face, that breath I can smell from way over
here. Awwww, you're still as cutey-wooty as you used
to be—except older and more zombie-ish. And
droolier. And dressed funny. Is that *you*, SCOODLY-
BOOT?!"

At first I was sure Super Vacation Man had lost his
mind. Then I realized he was probably right; although
Madame Zombina was an ugly lady, she was actually
kind of a cute dog.

"Scoodlyboot," cried the superhero, "it's me,
Super Vacation Man!"

"Me . . . no . . . know," she grunted.
"Me . . . no . . . care."

CHAPTER 24

SUPER NINCOMPOOP MAN

Super Vacation Man was an emotional wreck. He cared so much about Scoodlyboot and Blunder Mutt, and he felt he had let them both down.

Mondo Grumpo sprang into action, shaking his finger.

"Shame on you, Super Vacation Man! You lied! You fibbed! You've lost two dogs! Bad best friend! Bad superhero! Just plain bad!"

He shook his finger violently, sending moldy, yellow-green, negative lightning bolts flying.

"THE EVIL FINGER MAKES YOU
    SHIVER;
YOUR SWEAT AND TEARS RUN LIKE
    A RIVER;
YOU FEEL BAD RIGHT DOWN TO
    YOUR LIVER . . .
BAD, BAD BOY!!!"

Super Vacation Man melted and dripped off the chandelier, landing with a splash in the puddle of his own tears on the floor at Mondo Grumpo's feet. What an un-super way to go.

But of course, Mondo hadn't finished with him yet.

He scraped Super Vacation Man off the floor and squeezed moldy, supersour lemon juice all over him. Then he pushed and smooshed him around. It made a sickening squishing sound. It was a horrible thing to watch. He re-formed Super Vacation Man into a dead-eyed Nincompoop of Numbness.

"How do you feel now?" said Mondo.

"Me no feel nuthin'," he grunted.

"Perfect," said Mondo Grumpo.

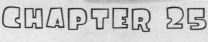

CHAPTER 25

Mondo Wacko

"**P**erfectly insane," I said.

"Insanely perfect!" he replied.

Then he explained his evil plot. He was more wacko than I thought. A lot more wacko.

"Okay," he said, "try to keep up: I'm going to use your Techno Helmet and techno brain to videoconference together all the guests, workers, and students of all the hotels, workplaces, and schools worldwide so I can turn them all into Nincompoops of Numbness. I will replace fun with dullness and boredom all over the world. No more vacations! School, three hundred and sixty-five days a year! Three hundred and sixty-*six* in leap year! Wait . . . ! I'm in charge! *Every* year will be leap year! And, let's see, school will last twenty-three point nine hours a day! That's just six minutes for sleep . . . six minutes for dreaming dull dreams of nincompoopishness! And no recess, no lunch breaks, no joking around with friends or teachers. I'll fire any teacher with an ounce of fun or niceness! Hee-hee . . . No, Grumpo! No laughing! Laughing bad! Lemons! Now!"

Mondo Grumpo ate a bushel of moldy, supersour lemons. The juice and peels flew like grass out of a lawnmower.

"And *you*, Amazing Techno Doofus. You're supposed to be the brainy one, but boy, is *that* way off! Trying to fool me with that idiotic beard! I mean, it doesn't even *look* like a beard. Looks more like a bad toupee! And, by the way—look around—all of this is your fault. Sure, *I* may have turned all these idiots into nincompoops, but let's face it, I'm just doing my job! And, let me think, what's *your* job? Oh, that's right . . . saving the day!

"So help me out here," he said. "We both have jobs—but who's doing his job *better*?"

He had a point. He was definitely doing his job better. Even though I knew what he was up to—saying nasty things to make me feel terrible— it was working. I felt really terrible. Out of focus. I looked at my hands. I could see through them. It was happening again.

I was breaking up into grainy, flickering blips and bleeps! This is my main weakness as a superhero. When I'm feeling bad or don't know what to do, my signal goes bad, like a TV or computer losing its connection. I turn into video snow. Mondo must have known this. He knew he could get to me this way.

"Now, if you don't mind," said Grumpo, "I need to borrow your Techno powers. And your BRAIN!"

CHAPTER 26
Amazing Techno Who?

"**P**repare yourself for numb nincompoopism!" he said. And he shook his finger, shooting moldy, yellow-green, negative lightning bolts right at me. I was too weak and out of focus to resist him now.

"THE EVIL FINGER MAKES YOU
    SHIVER;
YOUR SWEAT AND TEARS RUN LIKE
    A RIVER;
YOU FEEL BAD RIGHT DOWN TO
    YOUR LIVER ... BAD, BAD ..."

Just then, the real Skippy the TV Repair Boy wandered into the lobby. He looked lost.

"Excuse me," he said in a shaky, high-pitched voice, "which way to the National TV Repairman Convention?"

Mondo Grumpo did not like being interrupted.

"WHO DARES INTERRUPT THE EVIL FINGER SHAKE OF SHAME?!" he thundered.

Skippy shook like a leaf. Mondo looked at Skippy, then at me. He raised an eyebrow.

"Wait a minute," he said to Skippy. "You can't fool me. *You* are the real Amazing Techno Dude! *You* are the one in disguise! Your beard looks even *faker*! His at least looks something like human *hair*! Yours looks like a dead squirrel or a pile of lint or something!" He aimed his electro-charged finger at the terrified teenager.

Poor Skippy, or whatever his real name was.

He was just the wrong kid
in the wrong costume at the
wrong time. Now he was shaking
like a leaf in an earthquake.

He opened his mouth and
tried to say, "Excuse me,
sir? I am not Amazing
Techno Dude. So,
if you don't
mind, I'll just   go home now. Okay? Thank
you. Thank you very much."

But he was so scared, it came out like this: "Koooz-
z-z-I-I-grr-grr-ftt-ftt-homina-homina-
na-na-zaykoo-zaykoo-muff-muff."

"Easy for you to say," said somebody.

"Sounds like you've been taking
speech lessons from Blunder Mutt,"
said somebody else.

It was actually two connected
somebodies. And, funny thing: they
both had TV heads.

He/they looked at Mondo Grumpo
and he looked at them.

"First of all, Mr. Mondo," said Biff and Smiff, "those other fakey mcfakesters are fake. Second of all, *we* are the real Amazing Techno Dude, so borrow *our* brains! And third, find us a fresh diaper! And fourth, *right now*! And fifth, *we're serious*! And sixth, and most importantly, we saw Super Vacation Man and Blunder Mutt first, so we win the contest and now we are Amazing Techno Dude's new sidekick or kicks!"

Mondo Grumpo, of course, had no idea what they were talking about. "I thought you said *you* were Amazing Techno Dude. How can you be him and also be his *sidekick*? That's the stupidest thing I've ever heard! And I've heard a lot of stupid things!"

"Um . . . yes, well. Speaking of things," said Biff. "That's one of the *amazing things* about Amazing Techno Dude," said Smiff. "One of his/our powers is that he/we are able to be him/us *and* his/our sidekick at the same time!"

"Okay . . ." said Mondo

Grumpo. "But I've seen pictures of Amazing Techno Dude in the newspapers and I'm quite sure I would remember two heads. It's not like forgetting somebody's eye color or something."

Just then, *another* TV-headed person stepped up. This one's voice was more girlish: "Way wrong! *I* am Amazing Techno Dude and his new sidekick! Totally borrow *my* brain!"

"Hmmm," said Mondo. "It also seems that I would remember that girlish voice. And the skirt."

"I know," she squealed, "isn't it too cute?! I got it for forty percent off at the super-mall!"

"Excuse me?" said Mondo.

"Um . . . totally never mind," she replied. "Just borrow my brain!"

And then another.

"No, *me* Amazing Techno Dude and sidekick! My brain!"

That one looked curiously like a large rock inside a TV set, floating in the air.

"Now I *know* I'd remember that!" said Mondo.

He knew something was very wrong, but at this point he couldn't quite remember what the heck Amazing Techno Dude was supposed to look like.

They kept coming. One made bad puns. Another made predictions and flew around the room. Another made sarcastic remarks in an English accent. The last one just looked like a TV sitting on the floor with lots of sparks and "yee-haws" coming out of it.

Mondo Grumpo was surrounded by Amazing Techno Dudes who said they were also Amazing Techno Dude's sidekick and that he could borrow their brains!

SuperSass CuteGirl had gotten all the TVs at the mall.

"They think I'm just a shopaholic," she whispered to me, "but, like, duh, I just saved the day."

In fact, all the Super Goofballs were risking their lives for me! I was touched by this show of support. I was coming back into focus. I felt much better.

CHAPTER 27
Attack?

Meanwhile, Mondo Grumpo was feeling much worse. He was very, very confused. He looked from goofball to goofball, aiming his moldy yellow-green finger at one and then another. He didn't know which of us was the real Amazing Techno Dude.

But I knew exactly who I was. And I knew what I had to do.

I was still chained to that stupid chandelier, but I had an idea. I looked across the room at one of the TV sets, the one that was flying around with feathers shooting out of it: Pooky. I decided to *think* my idea to her so she could get the message to the others, by way of her Two-Way Mind-Reading Powers.

"Pooky! Testing, testing! Can you hear me? Listen. Don't worry about breaking my chains. Waste of time—they're superhero-proof. I've got an idea, though. Since Mondo Grumpo hates fun, we'll use fun as a weapon against him. And all those numb nincompoops who can't feel anything or care about anything? Maybe the power of pure fun will snap them out of it. So, Pooky, tell the other goofballs to think of a way to make that happen. Now!"

I wasn't sure if Pooky had heard me. Before I could think something like, "Pooky, did you hear me?", Mondo Grumpo called to his nincompoops.

"Enough with trying to figure out who's the real Amazing Techno Dude!" he cried. "I say we just defeat them all!"

Then he made the "Sign of the Frown" by putting his fingers in an upside-down "U" shape, signaling to his

nincompoop army to pre-
pare for battle.

The nincompoops
grunted and drooled. I
had never heard so much
grunting and drooling.

The goofballs looked
nervous. All that grunt-
ing and drooling was
pretty creepy.

"Attention warriors in
the Moldy Order of Numb
Nincompoopness!" Mondo
shouted. "ATTACK!"

But nothing happened.
"I said ATTACK!
ATTACK, *ATTACK,*
YOU NINCOM-
POOPS!"

But they didn't
attack. They didn't do
much of anything. It
hadn't occurred to this
so-called supergenius

that numb nincompoops don't really *care* enough about anything to actually *do* anything. They just stumbled around, bumping into one another, grunting and drooling.

CHAPTER 28

WIRED FOR NINCOMPOOPISM

ondo Grumpo was furious. He frowned so hard that his face turned twenty shades of yellow-green and moldy lemon juice gushed out of his ears.

He got down on his hands and knees and crawled across the room, around and through the legs of the stumbling nin- compoops. He untied the rope and lowered me down from the

chandelier. He
took a close look
at me. Really close. I
could see moldy hairs
growing out of his moldy
nostrils. I almost passed out from
his moldy breath.

"I'm pretty sure that you are the real
Amazing Techno Dude," he said.

Then he grabbed the end of the chain I was
wrapped in and dragged me across the room. The
Super Goofballs tried to stop him, but they got tangled in the huge crowd of stumbling, grunting
droolers.

Mondo Grumpo dragged me into the manager's
office and slammed and locked the door. It was very
quiet in there. He said the door was soundproof, so
there was no point in yelling for my goofball friends.
The room was dark, too. The only light was the

yellow-green glow of Mondo's face. "That's better," he said. "I need a little peace and quiet when I give evil speeches. I love giving evil speeches."

"I hadn't noticed that," I said.

"First, my evil biography: Once upon a time there was a wonderfully grumpy evil genius . . ."

Oh, brother. I hoped Pooky was using my plan, but I couldn't hear anything through that soundproof door. I had to do something. I decided to try my High-Definition Video-Zombie Hypno-Stare on him. I tried to think of a really bad TV show, something happy and silly that's really stupid but makes you laugh.

I had it: *Mr. Happy's Silly, Silly, Stupid Show.* It was only on for half a season when I was little, but boy did it make me laugh in a very stupid way. Guaranteed to turn Mondo into a babbling video-zombie.

I gathered all my energy, snapped my head back,

and shouted, *"Hypno-Stare, on!"*

A scorching blue video ray leaped from my eyes, right at Mondo Grumpo.

But he was ready for it. He whipped out a pair of special Anti-Amazing-Techno-Dude-High-Definition-Video-Zombie-Hypno-Stare Protective Glasses and put them on. He really had done his homework.

The ray just bounced off. The Hypno-Stare was totally useless against him.

This was not good.

"Hmmm . . ." he said in a supersnotty tone, "that would have tickled a bit, if I were ticklish. But, where was I? Oh, yes . . . Experts agree that the words 'evil' and 'genius' don't even begin to describe this evil genius's evil genius!" he said.

Man, this guy loved to hear himself talk. And as he talked, he attached a thick cable to the back of my TV helmet. The cable led to a moldy machine called the Grumpo-Nincomputer. From that, bigger cables ran up the wall and through a large hole in the roof. I could see rows of huge satellite dishes up there. They had blinking, moldy, yellow-green lights on them. The satellite dishes were humming and sizzling.

". . . and while attending evil-genius school," he continued, "this remarkable evil genius got per- fect scores on all the evil genius stan- dardized tests. Pretty good, eh?"

"Good for *nothing*," I said.

"Oh yeah, Not-At-All-Amazing Dude? Well, speaking of good and nothing, *nothing* you say now will do you any *good*. Because it's showtime. Using your TV head and brain, I'll send out a signal so powerful, it'll get to everybody on earth with a television set or computer. Phones and videogames, too. And did you ever hear about those people who can hear radio signals through the fillings in their teeth? It's like their head becomes a radio. Sounds crazy, but it's true! I'll get my message to those people, too. Aren't I deliciously evil? Don't I bring delicious evilness to the level of art? I mean, sure, I'm a mad *scientific* genius, that goes without saying. But I think I'm a mad *artistic* genius, too! Like Vincent Van Grumpo or something, don't you think?"

"I think you talk too much," I said.

"Well, you know what? After one flip of this switch, *you* won't be doing a lot of thinking *or* talking. I was going to turn you into a numb nincompoop first, but I changed my mind. I'd like you *not* to be numb for what comes next!"

CHAPTER 29

Friends to the End

"**A**nd who cares what you think anyway?" Grumpo said.

He pressed a button, an electric door slid open, and there stood Super Vacation Man and Blunder Mutt. They were both still in a grunting, drooling daze.

"Me . . . no . . . care . . . 'bout . . . nuthin'," grunted Blunder Mutt.

"Me . . . no . . . care . . . 'bout . . . nuthin' . . . neither," drooled Super Vacation Man.

"Oh, wow," said Mondo Grumpo, "I wish I wanted to laugh my head off. The idea of these two not caring about you is too hilarious!"

He waved his hands in Blunder's face.

"Hey, man's best friend! Look over here! Man in trouble! Actually, *two* men in trouble!"

He snapped his fingers so close, he was touching Blunder's nose.

"YOOHOO! MAN'S BEST FRIEND! Look at that—NOTHING!"

But actually, something was stirring inside Blunder Mutt. Somewhere down deep—maybe in his heart, maybe in his head, maybe in his belly—his supercanine instincts were waking up.

He sniffed the air.

Then blinked.

Then blinked and sniffed and sniffed and blinked.

Then he tried to speak.

"Mazz . . . bezz . . .

frezz?" said Blunder Mutt.

"Oh, look," said Mondo Grumpo, "the numb nincompooper is trying to speak."

"Mazz . . . bezz . . . frezz? Mazz . . . bezz . . . frezz?"

"Blunder, are you in there?" I said.

"Souptezz Vacazezz Mazz?!" said Blunder Mutt.

"No, it's Amazing Techno Dude," I said. "But Super Vacation Man is here, too!"

"Are you crazy?" said Mondo Grumpo. "He's speaking gibberish!"

"No!" I said. "He's speaking about as good as he *ever* speaks!"

Blunder turned slowly toward Super Vacation Man. He blinked and sniffed some more.

Then something clicked

in his head. I actually heard it click, like a rusted gear starting up.

His eyes opened. This pup was not the kind of nincompoop who could stay numb for long.

"Soupter Vacazy Man?!" he cried.

Blunder leaped onto Super Vacation Man and started licking his face. It was like the dog version of mouth-to-mouth resuscitation. And it was starting to work.

Mondo looked on in horror. He didn't even try to stop Blunder. For a disgusting guy, Mondo was very disgusted by dog slobber. It represented happiness to him, which, of course, he wanted to avoid.

Super Vacation Man was getting a little better, but he

was still about three-quarters nincompoop.

Then Blunder licked inside his ears, and that did the trick. A dog slobbering inside your ears is guaranteed to bring you back from the deepest, darkest nincompoopism.

"Blunder Mutt, is that you?" Super Vacation Man laughed.

"Yes, yes, yessy-yes!"

He rubbed Blunder's belly and they both laughed and howled. Then I laughed and howled. Which made Mondo Grumpo really, really angry.

CHAPTER 30

COUNTDOWN TO INTERNATIONAL NINCOMPOOPISM

"**E**nough of this licking and laughing and acting all happy! If you move a muscle, I'll zap you with my finger again!" said Mondo Grumpo. "Back to the evil business at hand! And by that, I mean back to flipping the switch and doing the whole 'Death of Fun' thing!"

He put his finger on the switch.

He held a microphone in his other hand. A camera was pointed at him. He was ready for the big videoconference.

People all over the world were about to get his message of evil grumpiness. They'd all be numb nincompoops in a matter of seconds!

"Mr. Grumpo, sir—how about a countdown?" I asked. "Countdowns are always nice." I figured it would buy me a little time.

"Good idea, very evil genius-y," said Mondo. "Here we go: twenty, nineteen, eighteen . . ."

I wasn't really sure what I could do. I was bound in chains. My remote was smashed to bits. I didn't have a clue.

"Seventeen, sixteen . . . you know what?" said Grumpo. "I just remembered that I really hate these long countdowns. I hate them in movies and I hate them in real life. There's no point to them. And so: three, two, one . . . BLAH, BLAH, BLAH . . . LONG LIVE GRUMPINESS!"

He flipped the switch.

A huge flash flashed, showering sparks all over the room. He looked into the camera and spoke into the microphone.

"Testing, one, two, three . . . GREETINGS, FUTURE NINCOMPOOPS!"

He pointed his finger at the camera and spoke to the world.

"THE EVIL FINGER MAKES YOU
    SHIVER;
  YOUR SWEAT AND TEARS RUN LIKE
    A RIVER . . ."

I looked over at Super Vacation Man and the scared
look on his face made *me* scared. It was the kind of
look that said, "Oh well, it looks like we're all—*zap,
zing, frizzle*—doomed."

"YOU FEEL BAD RIGHT DOWN TO
  YOUR LIVER . . ."

But Blunder Mutt didn't look
scared at all. And for a generally
confused guy, he didn't even look
confused.

He put his finger on his
forehead and said, "Must
do the thinky thing!"

But then he put that same finger
in the air and shouted, *"No! No time
for the thinky thing! Must do the
doing thing!* But first, the catchy

phrase: WHOLE WIDE WORLDY, HEAR ME
CALL ... BLUNDER NUT BE SAVE YOU ALL!"

He opened his mouth really wide and dove across
the room. He landed mouth-first on the huge cable
and chomped down. Teeth scattered across the floor.
He growled through his remaining teeth and huge
sparks flew. Those earlier sparks were hardly even
sparks compared to these sparks. It sounded like a hundred lightning bolts were crashing at the same time.

Blunder lit up like the Fourth of July. Fireworks
exploded from his nose. His tail spun like a propeller
and his ears flapped like a hummingbird's wings,

which lifted him like a furry little airplane. He began to rotate around the cable, doing somersaults in midair. He kept biting and growling and somersaulting. He sounded like some kind of crazy power tool.

Kids: do not try this at home. Or even away from home.

But, at last, he cut through the cable. It ripped apart and flopped to the floor, crackling and wiggling like electric eels in pain.

Blunder dropped to the floor with a thud.

Everything stopped. The fireworks, the screeching, the roaring, the growling . . . everything.

Smoke was pouring out of Mondo Grumpo's camera and microphone. I looked up and saw that the satellite dishes had all melted.

Blunder was lying on his back with his legs sticking straight up in the air. His feet were smoking like chimneys.

CHAPTER 31

Blunder, Blunder!
Wherefore Art Thou, Blunder?

Blunder Mutt looked like a furry toasted marshmallow. How does he always manage to get himself blown up? So brave. So dumb. So Blunderish. So Muttish.

"Blunder Mutt!" shouted Super Vacation Man. "Are you all right?"

One of Blunder's eyes popped open. Then the other. His head popped up.

"Blun . . . Blun . . . Blun," he said. He couldn't even say his own name. Every time he said "Blun" a little puff of smoke came out of his mouth.

"Blun . . . Blun . . . Blun . . ."

It seemed like maybe from now on, all he would

ever say was "Blun."

But then he said more.

"Blun . . . der . . . woulda . . . paid . . . a . . . lotta . . . money for that. If Blunder *hadda* lotta money. 'Cause dat was da most fun Blunder ever had. Ever. Ever."

Mondo Grumpo was too dumbfounded to speak.

"Well, I can think of something that might be even *more* fun," I said. "What do you say we take care of a certain grumpy supervillain?"

"I say what are we— *yo, uh-huh, go-go-go*—waiting for?" said Super Vacation Man.

"Me say that same azack ting!" said Blunder.

Mondo Grumpo took off running, and we took off chasing him. We all crashed through the soundproof door and into the lobby.

CHAPTER 32
The Final Battle

We were hit by a gigantic wave of music and laughter. A huge party-battle was in full swing. Man, was it loud in there. Pooky had apparently gotten my message to the others and the goofballs were battling the numb nincompoops with the power of pure fun. Mondo was now surrounded by goofballs, so Blunder, Super Vacation Man, and I sat down and enjoyed the show.

SuperSass Cutegirl was playing very loud music through a very tiny ring on her finger. She was holding her hand up in a fist above her head and every color of the rainbow was shooting out of the ring, filling the lobby with music and wild, swirling lights. It was music I'd never heard before—a combination of all styles, adding up to pure musical madness. But good madness. And it was all coming from this tiny ring.

"To get into the battle groove, you need something with a beat that's easy to battle to," said SuperSass.

All the super roommates were twitching. And tapping. And bouncing and bopping to the beat. Biff and Smiff knocked their heads together. Wonder Boulder broke himself in two and knocked his two halves together.

Mondo Grumpo's eye started twitching along with the beat. He couldn't control himself. His body was desperately trying to have fun even though his brain kept saying that it hated fun.

"YOUNG LADY!" said Mondo Grumpo, "TURN OFF THAT RING!"

SuperSass turned it up.

The Frankenstein Punster made jokes to the beat:

"WHAT USE FROZEN BANDAIDS FOR?"
"COLDCUTS. HA, HOO, HA."
"WHAT WHALES CHEW?"
"BLUBBER GUM. HA, HOO, HA!"

Hotel guests started laughing. The kids laughed so hard that milk gushed from their noses— milk they'd had for breakfast hours earlier. Their parents gushed coffee.

Mighty Tighty Whitey scooped up eight nincompoops and crammed them

inside himself,
like clowns in a clown car,
and then bungee jumped around
the room to the beat. He looked pretty
funny with sixteen legs sticking through his leg
holes.

Wonder Boulder broke out of his TV set, wrapped three nincompoop kids in his cape, and blasted through the wall to the outside. They flew out over the beach and dove down into the ocean. Then they exploded out of the water with a bunch of fish and octopi hanging on for dear life. Then they skipped along the surface like a skipping stone. Dolphins leaped and laughed along with them. Finally, when Wonder crashed back into the hotel lobby, all three kids were screaming, "YIPPEEEEEEEEE!"

But T-Tex3000 was still inside his TV, racing around the lobby, crashing into things and yelling "yee-haw." I was beginning to wonder if he had any super usefulness at all.

In fact, all the goofballs looked like they were running out of steam. There were simply too many Nincompoops of Numbness!

I realized there was really only one man for this job: Super Vacation Man.

"SVM," I said, "I think they need your . . . help."

"Did someone say the 'H' word?" he replied.

Then he took a deep breath—so deep he sucked all the air out of the room for a moment, his chest expanding to ten times its normal size— then shouted in his deepest, super-est possible voice:

"ANYTIME AND
ANY*WHERE*,
CALL FOR HELP AND I'LL
BE THERE!
I PROMISE!
BUT FIRST THINGS FIRST!"

He scooped up Scoodlyboot and took her on a vacation-powered ride so wild, it quickly cured her of her numb nincompoopism. It was probably the triple backwards twisting flip off the hotel balcony in the motorboat that did it. Scoodlyboot's memories came rushing back. A huge grin spread over her furry face. She stopped grunting and drooling and started howling and laughing.

"Super Vacation *Man*?!"

"Scoodly-Scoodly-boot-boot-boot?!"

Then Super Vacation Man used every one of his powers—supersurfing, superbackstroking in midair, super-everything vacation-y—to thrill nincompoop after nincompoop out of numbness. He even used his super lazin'-by-the-pool power.

He cured dozens
and dozens of nin-
compoops in fast-motion
throughout the resort: by
boat, by bike, by Jet Ski, all
over the lobby, in the pool,
on the badminton and shuffle-
board courts, in the sauna, on the
beach—bouncing off of a large sunbathing lady in a

small bikini (*"Not you again!"*)— through the rooms, the bath-rooms, the boiler rooms . . . everywhere!

In no time, all of the hotel work-ers and guests had been rescued from numbness.

We lifted Super Vacation Man on our shoulders and cheered.

The party-battle was over. Now it was just a party-party.

CHAPTER 33

Grumpo's Getaway

Mondo Grumpo decided to sneak out while he still could. I looked over just in time to see him climbing aboard the fancy, moldy, golden green luggage cart. He stood on top of the suitcases and shouted really, really loudly, "SO LONG, YOU STUPID, SICKENING SMILERS!"

Mondo shouted so loudly that, not only did everyone stop what they were doing, the sound waves caused SuperSass's ring to explode.

Which stopped the music. Which stopped the party.

Mondo took out his moldy, yellow-green key and started the Fancy, Moldy Golden Green Luggage

Cart's engines. Then a helicopter propeller pushed up and out of the pile of suitcases!

It was now the Mondo Grumpo Nincompoopter, and it lifted slowly off the floor in a blast of moldy, yellow-green flame and smoke, powered by supersour grump-powered lemon rocket fuel.

Mondo Grumpo made the "Sign of the Frown" and shouted over the roar of the engines: "Listen, you freaky fun-sters! You've won the battle, but I will win the grumpy war! For, mark my grumpy words: I'LL BE BACK—GRUMPIER THAN EVER—AND THE WORLD, NO, THE UNIVERSE, WILL BEND TO MY GRUMPY WILL, AND EVERYONE WILL LIVE NUMB-NINCOMPOOPIER EVER AFTER!"

Even Mondo's farewell speech was way too long.

But he was actually getting away. The Nincompoopter was rising toward the hole in the roof. Then, out of the corner of my eye, I saw a TV set racing along the floor.

There was an explosion of sparks, a big *"yee-haw,"* and a mechanical lasso came blasting through its screen. The lasso zigzagged across the room—up, down, left, right, around goofballs and ex-nincompoops, through legs, over heads, around chairs and couches—until it reached Mondo Grumpo. Over his head it went. It slid around his shoulders, wriggled down his body, and around his legs. And then T-Tex3000 yanked on it from inside his TV set and the mechanical rope pulled tight around Mondo's ankles. T-Tex3000 turned out to be super useful after all.

Mondo struggled to stay standing, teetering atop the suitcases.

"Oh, Mr. Mondo!" I called. "You must admit, you're looking kinda funny now."

"NO!" he said, "I'M NOT FUNNY AND I NEVER *LOOK* FUNNY!"

Then Mighty Tighty Whitey slingshot himself across the lobby and landed on top of Mondo Grumpo's head. He stomped on his bald spot a few times and then stretched himself over his face. Mondo was looking out through one of the leg holes and Mighty's arms and legs were wiggling in the air.

HA! HA! HA! HA! HA! HA! HA! HA! HA! HA!

Everybody cracked up.

Just then, Scoodlyboot accidentally stepped on a tiny piece of my shattered remote. A blinding flash created a large cloud of smoke, and a young, beautiful dog emerged. Scoodlyboot had shot through time and returned a whole lot younger. I mean, she was like a canine supermodel. And for some unknown reason, she took one look at Blunder Mutt and fell deeply in love. She expressed that love with a bit of poetry:

"Roses are red,
   Cashew's a nut,
   I love a Blunder,
   Whose last name is Mutt."

Unfortunately, Blunder didn't feel the same.
   He also didn't like the poem.
   "Sorry, sis . . . a soupy brave hero-ish dog such as
me jes' got no time for lovely ladies or stinkish poem-
ses in my dizzy schedule!"

CHAPTER 34
super payback Man

Meanwhile, Super Vacation Man was hovering above Mondo Grumpo like he was treading water without the water. He glared down at the miserable creep who had stolen his Scoodlyboot and ruined his vacation.

Mondo was terrified. This was his worst fear: the recreational wrath of Super Vacation Man.

Super Vacation Man looked Mondo Grumpo in

the eye and chanted a chant that sounded familiar, yet
different:

"VACATION POWER WILL MAKE YOU
    SWEAT;
A FLIP, A FLOATEE—
   YOU'RE ALL WET;
     THE FUN YOU HATE IS THE
          FUN YOU'LL
          GET;
           LAUGH!
           LAUGH!
           LAUGH!"

Mondo Grumpo
turned into a quiver-
ing pile of giggling,
jiggling jelly and slid down
the pile of suitcases to the floor. The Nincompooper
took off through the hole in the roof without him.

Super Vacation Man scooped Mondo Grumpo up
and molded him into a slightly less grumpy Mondo
Grumpo. Then he took him on a super tour of fun.

"NO! PLEASE!" Mondo cried and laughed as he

was dragged through the door, "NOT LAZIN' BY THE POOL! ANYTHING BUT LAZIN' BY THE POOL!"

He snapped his fingers, but all the moldy, super-sour lemons in the world couldn't save him now. Everyone cheered really, really loudly. So loudly, in fact, that the sound waves restarted SuperSass's ring, which started the music, which restarted the party.

The goofballs wanted to know about the whole sidekick thing. (*"Me! Me! Me!"*). I told them that since they all helped find Super Vacation Man and Blunder Mutt, I would give them each a try on one mission apiece before I made my final decision.

I called the Gritty City Police and Sergeant Bub McButt came in a flash to pick up Mondo Grumpo. I wasn't sure what punish-ment would be right for him. He might actually *like* jail.

CHAPTER 35
SPITTLEMAN SPAULDING OF RETURN THE?

Just then, a very fancy car crashed through the revolving door and into the lobby. Backwards. A certain backwards lady got out with a certain Mr. Spaulding Spittleman. The *real* Spaulding Spittleman—her new boyfriend. His face was as white as a sheet and his hair was standing straight up.

The car was very badly dented. Spittleman had made the mistake of letting Granny drive.

"What on earth is going on here?" he cried, staring at his destroyed hotel.

The nervous employees explained what had happened.

"My hotel is totaled," said Spittleman. "Well, at least the car can be fixed."

Just then, the gigantic floor buffer came roaring back into the lobby and ran over Spittleman's car, squashing it like a bug.

"Well, maybe not," he said. "But, you know, I have a lot to be thankful for. All you good people saved the world from grumpiness and numb nincompoopism.

Which is a very, very good thing. To celebrate, I'm treating everyone to a free vacation!"

"Yippee!" said all the Super Goofballs and ex-nincompoops.

Spittleman turned out to be a nice guy. He was a whole lot nicer than Mondo Grumpo pretending to be him. When he smiled, he meant it. And he only spit a tiny bit when he talked.

So everyone got a vacation, except Super Vacation Man, who had broken his funny bone and lots of other bones during the battle. Turns out playing fetch with two crazy dogs, while riding a Jet Ski upside down, while juggling beach balls, while reading a magazine, while putting on suntan lotion, while drinking a drink with a little umbrella in it, is not all that safe.

Super Vacation Man spent an entire week in traction in his hotel room. He listened to everyone's tales of their fabulous vacation. We drew pictures of our adventures all over his full-body cast, which he looked at longingly with a system of mirrors I built for him.

CHAPTER 36

HOME IS WHERE THE TROPHIES ARE

inally, we returned home, where we found a note on the front door:

Dear Blunder Mutt:
What's up? I hear you were looking for me! I live right next door. I play the guitar, but my band just broke up. If you and your goofball buddies feel like getting a band together, just let me know. By the way, I'm also looking for a place to practice.
    sincerely,
The Invisible Superbad Blue-Fanged Ferret

"Oh yeah, I've heard of him," I said. "He's a famous musician."

"I knew I knew that name from somewhere," said Super Vacation Man.

"Well, I am a heckuva goodish music type guy, too," said Blunder Mutt.

"Count me in, mate!" said Mighty Tighty Whitey.

"Rock to born was I!" said you-know-who.

"Me actually *born* a *rock*," said another you-know-who.

"Don't forget *me*!"

And all the me-ing started again.

Blunder phoned the Invisible Super-bad Blue-Fanged Ferret to come over and start practicing with us in the practice room, which we used to call the basement.

I was too tired to fight it. Besides, I had always wanted to start a band. I wouldn't have chosen these exact band members, but you work with what you have.

A city truck pulled up and dumped hundreds of trophies and medals, as thanks from a grateful Gritty City, onto the front porch, which immediately collapsed. Then some people wandered by, assumed it was a yard sale, and bought a few trophies. I couldn't believe I'd never thought of that before. People will buy anything at a yard sale. They even bought pieces of the broken porch. Blunder Mutt sold one of his broken teeth.

And boy, we had enough trophies and medals to pay a *lot* of bills.

The phone rang. Blunder Mutt and Scoodlyboot *both* answered it. Actually, only Blunder was trying to answer the phone. Scoodlyboot was trying to kiss Blunder Mutt. The phone fell from their slobbery mouths and slid across the floor. Blunder spit like he'd tasted poison.

"Listen, lady!" he said. "Blunder's schedule still way, way, *way* too dizzy!"

I didn't really want to touch that slobbery phone, so I pressed speakerphone and said, "Hello, House of Super Goofballs, Amazing Techno Dude speaking."

"What?! You haven't *left* yet?!!!"

"You have *got* to be kidding," I said.

"Yes, I am kidding," said Mayor What's-His-Name.

"Funny," I said.

He said he had gotten a ransom note from Lousy Lou the LaundroManiac, who was holding Jumpin' Jack Jockstrap and the Battlin' Bra of Birmingham hostage.

"*No!!!*" cried Mighty Tighty Whitey. "*That's me mum and dad!*"

the super-goofy adventures continue in

SUPER GOOFBALLS #3
super underwear...and Beyond!

Mighty Terrible Situation

Mighty Tighty Whitey was one freaked-out pair of jockey shorts.

"Don't worry, Mum and Dad!" he shouted in his thick English accent, striking a super-heroic pose. *"I'm comin'!"*

Mayor What's-His-Name had just phoned to tell us that Lousy Lou the LaundroManiac had clothes-napped Jumpin' Jack Jockstrap and the Battlin' Bra of Birmingham, Mighty's superhero parents.

Mighty was mighty upset. He tensed up and his elastic waist/headband snapped shut. His face got bright red and hot air built up inside. The air had to go somewhere, and it pushed up and out, causing the elastic to vibrate, making a super high-pitched farting sound.

Blunder Mutt laughed so hard he fell on his face. He kept laughing as he stood up, dusted himself off, and fell on his face again.

Mighty Tighty Whitey was not amused. "I don't know what you find so bloomin' funny 'bout a supah bra and jockstrap gettin' clothesnapped!"

He whacked a nail into the floor with three super-fast hammer whacks. Then he stretched the backside of his waist/headband up over the front side, hooked it on the nail, dug in his heels and leaned back, stretching all the way across the room.

"Jeepers-freepers, I wishes I could be makin' myself longer an' longer all aways crosstah room!" said Blunder Mutt.

"I think our friend Blunder means to say he wishes he were *stretchy*," I said.

"No," Blunder replied, a little annoyed, "Blunder meanded to say jeepers-freepers, I wishes I could be makin' myself longer an' longer all aways crosstah room!"

"All right, all right . . . stand back!" shouted Mighty Tighty Whitey, straining hard against the super tension of his elastic. "Fantastic! Elastic! Sarcastic!"

But just as Mighty Tighty Whitey was about to let go and fly through the window, the nail ripped a gaping hole through the fabric of his forehead—if a pair of underwear actually *has* a forehead—and he flew backwards instead, into the kitchen-lair, and landed with a crash into the open dishwasher/3D electron probe analytic refractor. The impact caused the door to slam shut and the machine to turn on. We heard a muffled "Blubba flah-bubbah-boobly-floobly!" from inside.

The Goofballs went into superpanic mode.